This Walker book belongs to:

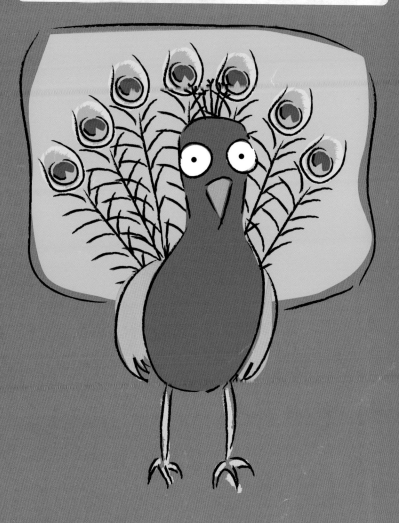

To our dads, who, along with our moms,
tucked us in with the best bedtime stories in the world

D. H. & S. S.

First published 2010 by Walker Books Ltd
87 Vauxhall Walk, London SE11 5HJ

This edition published 2013

2 4 6 8 10 9 7 5 3

© 2010 Dean Hacohen and Sherry Scharschmidt

The right of Dean Hacohen and Sherry Scharschmidt to be identified as author/
illustrators of this work has been asserted by them in accordance with the
Copyright, Designs and Patents Act 1988

This book has been typeset in Journal and Providence Sans

Printed in China

British Library Cataloguing in Publication Data:
a catalogue record for this book is available from the British Library

ISBN 978-1-4063-3203-2

www.walker.co.uk

Tuck Me In!

Dean Hacohen &
Sherry Scharschmidt

WALKER BOOKS
AND SUBSIDIARIES
LONDON · BOSTON · SYDNEY · AUCKLAND

It's time for bed.

Who needs to be tucked in?

I do!

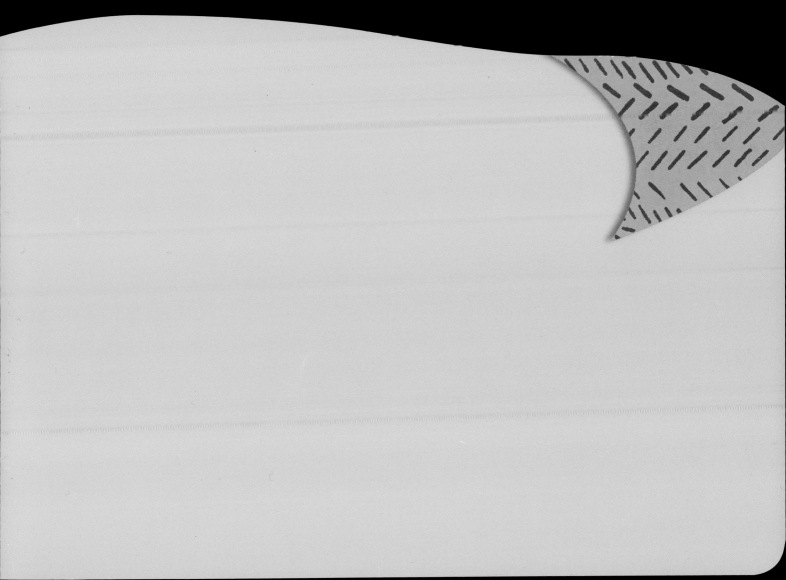

Goodnight, Baby Pig.

Who else needs to be tucked in?

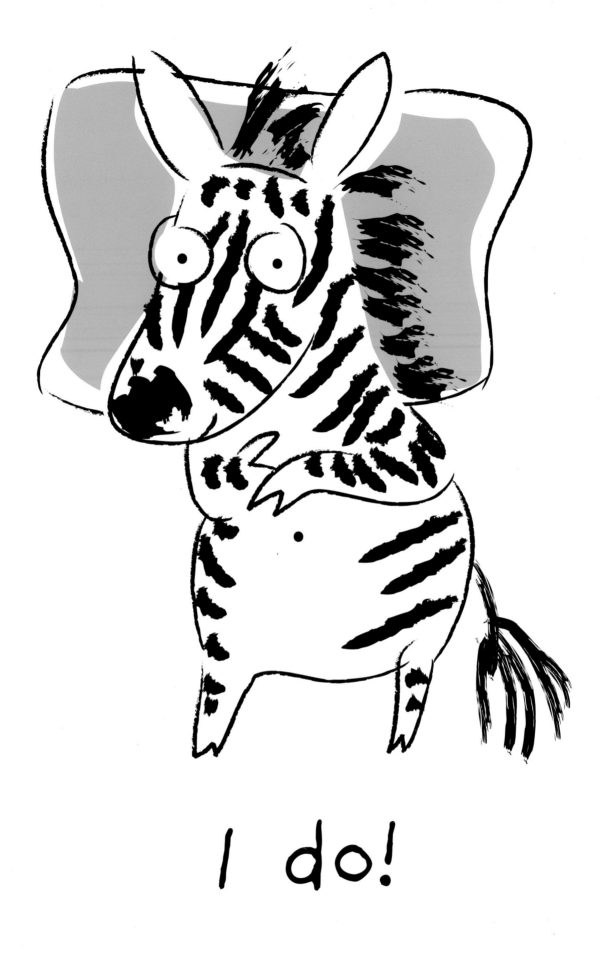

I do!

Goodnight, Baby Zebra.

Who else needs to be tucked in?

I do!

Goodnight, Baby Elephant.

Who else needs to be tucked in?

I do!

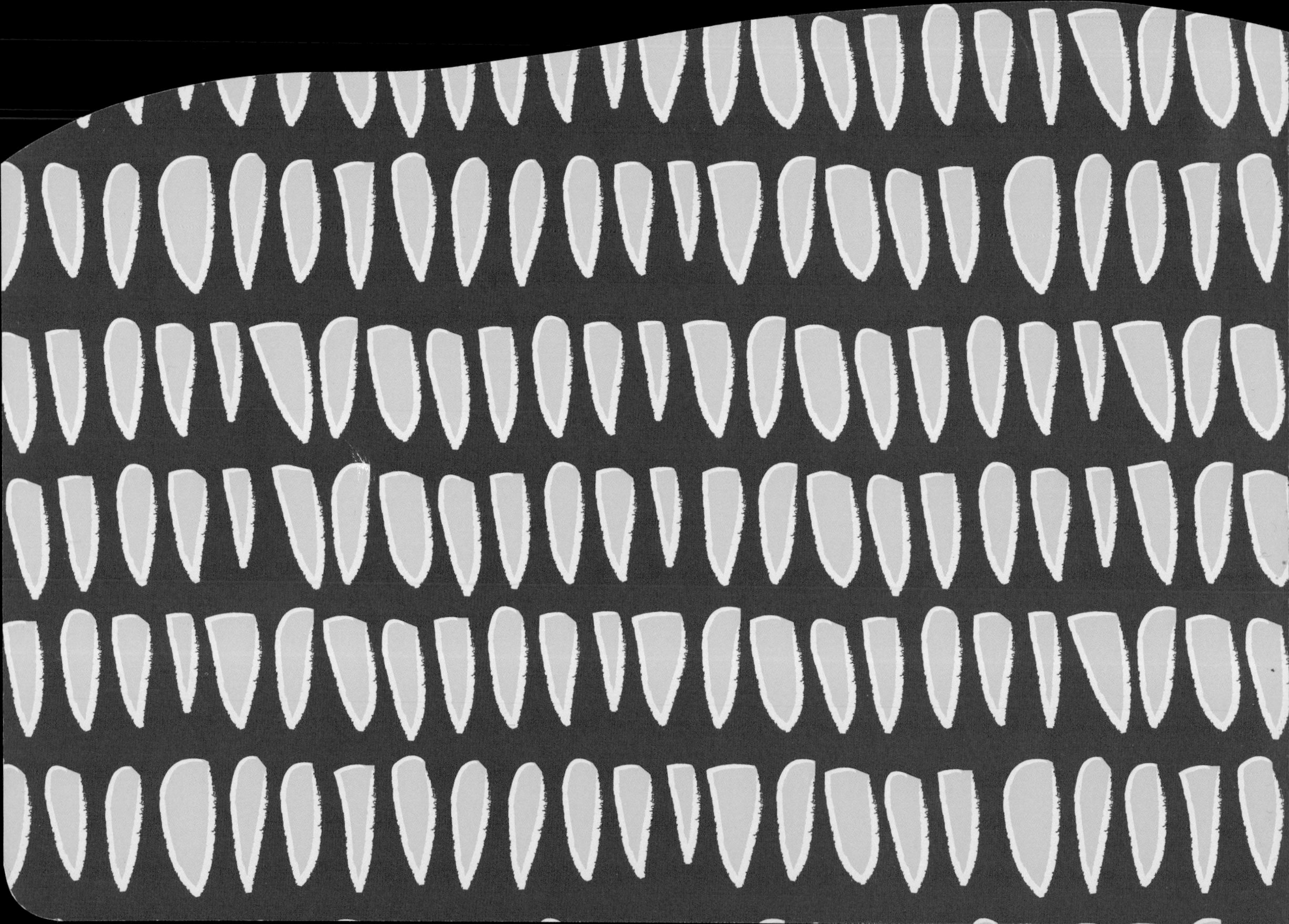

Goodnight, Baby Alligator.

Who else needs to be tucked in?

I do!

Goodnight, Baby Moose.

Who else needs to be tucked in?

I do!

Goodnight, Baby Hedgehog.

Who else needs to be tucked in?

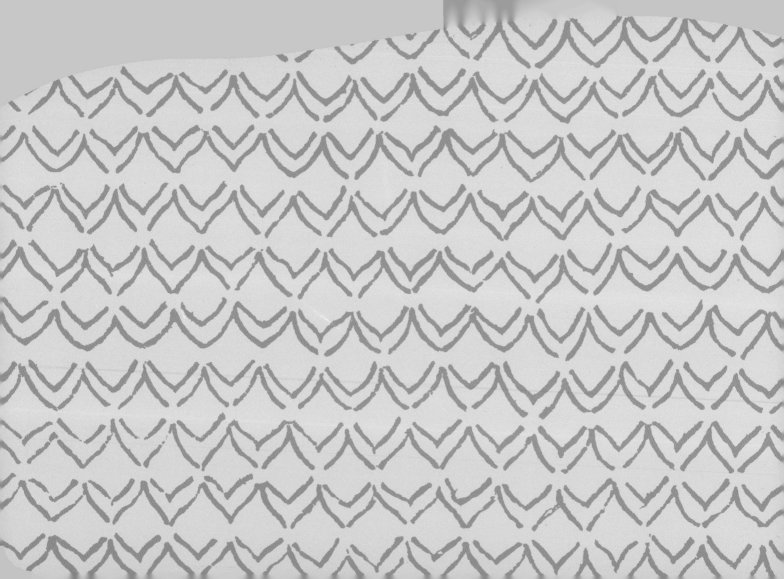

Goodnight, Baby Peacock.

Does anyone else need to be tucked in?

Do you?

Goodnight, **you!**

More bedtime stories from
Walker Books

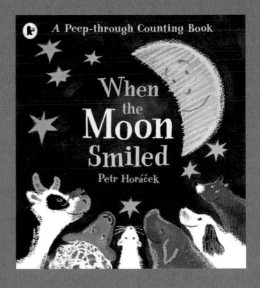

ISBN 978-1-4063-3612-2

ISBN 978-0-7445-7047-2

Available from all good booksellers

www.walker.co.uk